W9-CUC-732

For Ophelia,
    forever

THIS BOOK BELONGS TO

_____

Hello.
I hope you have fun in our little
corner of the world!
Very soon, you will meet Manoosh,
Baloosh, Nuno and all their
friends as they learn about our
wonderful world.
So until we meet again, look around.
The world is yours.

Lavinia

Copyright 2002 by Lavinia Branca Snyder.

A LAVINIA'S WORLD™ book in **The Little Stories of Manoosh and Baloosh**™ series.
Lavinia's World and The Little Stories of Manoosh and Baloosh are trademarks of
Lavinia Branca Snyder.
Published by Aurora Libris Corp., New York. All rights reserved.
Printed in China

Library of Congress Number: 2003104531
ISBN 1-932233-01-6

Text edited by Pam Pollack
Special thanks to Frank Palminteri
and, as always,
thank you Brian for being both my husband and my friend.

The Little Stories of
Manoosh & Baloosh

Going Home

Story by Lavinia Branca Snyder
Illustrations by Lavinia Branca Snyder
and
Emanuela Riccioni

Published by Aurora Libris Corp., New York

One sunny morning in Rainbowville, the little peas Manoosh and Baloosh were at school.

"Do you hear a noise?" Manoosh whispered to Baloosh.

"I wonder what Ms. Lucia brought today," said Baloosh.

"It sounds like someone's giggling," said Manoosh.

After school Manoosh and Baloosh looked behind Ms. Lucia's desk. They saw a big cactus and a little seed.

 Baloosh asked who they were. The little seed said his name was Nuno, and the big cactus was his aunt Mammilaria.

"We're the Ooshes," said Baloosh.

"Where do you come from?" asked Manoosh.

"Sonora," Nuno replied. "It's a hot, dry place with lots of cactuses. We came here for a visit, but now I'd like to go home. Can you take us there?"

"We'll ask our friend Balthazar to help us," Manoosh said. "We'll ask to borrow the big balloon he uses to travel all over the world."

The Ooshes took Nuno and his aunt to Balthazar's house. He was happy to lend his maps, his compass and his balloon so they could take Nuno home.

Manoosh, Baloosh and Nuno climbed into the basket of the great balloon. Manoosh piloted it up, up into the sky.

"This is wonderful," said Nuno. "We're floating through the clouds."

They floated over seas and mountains, carried by the winds. They flew down into a green leafy place. The air was hot and moist. They could see animals high up in the trees. Birds were singing everywhere.

"I think this is Amazonia," Baloosh said.

"Let's take a look around," said Manoosh and Nuno.

As they landed the balloon they passed a sloth sleeping in a tall tree. They said hello to Ant Betty and her sisters. "Hello," the leaf cutter ant triplets said all together.

Nuno laughed.

"Do you know that fellow in the tree?" Baloosh asked. "He must have a good view from up there."

"Follow us," said the triplets, running up the tree. "We'll introduce you to Lento."

"Have you seen any hot, dry cactus-y places?" Manoosh asked the sloth.

"No-o-o-pe." Lento said very slowly. "Go ask Rojo the rooster. He knows everything."

They walked through the jungle until they reached Rojo the rooster. They asked him if there were any cactuses around.

"Hmmm," Rojo said, "here in the Amazon jungle we have lots of rain, crocodiles, piranhas, birds... but I've never seen a cactus that looks like him."

"We'll keep looking," the Ooshes said. The sun was beginning to set, and the three friends took a nap. The next day they flew off at dawn.

In a few days and nights they had crossed the Atlantic Ocean. One morning they saw the desert. It was called "the Sahara" on Balthazar's map.

"It sure is hot and dry." said Nuno.

Manoosh landed the balloon but didn't see Spiny the hedgehog below them. He got out of the way fast.

"Hello there," she called out to a nearby caravan of camels. "Are there any cactuses like Nuno in this hot, dry place?"

"Well, I've traveled great distances across this desert," Khalif the camel replied, "but I've never seen any cactuses like Nuno. We're just leaving this oasis. I'll show you the way to Mrs. Fennec's."

"She's the wisest of foxes," said Spiny.

Nuno and the Ooshes followed Khalif across the dunes. A few hours later they reached Mrs. Fennec's. She was playing tag with her pups in the sand.

"Excuse me," said Baloosh. "Have you seen any cactuses like Nuno around here? He's from Sonora."

"I'm afraid not," Mrs. Fennec said. "But why don't you stay and play with us?"

Everyone played and laughed all day long. Then Nuno and the peas said goodbye and climbed back into the balloon.

They floated over Asia and the snowy Himalayan Mountains until they reached the blue Pacific Ocean.

They brought the balloon down on a hot, sandy island. Manoosh and Baloosh were surprised and happy to see their friend Flyer the dolphin jumping through the waves.

"Hi, Flyer," the two peas called.

"Hey, Manoosh and Baloosh, what are you doing in this part of the world?" asked Flyer.

"We're with our friend Nuno the seed and we're looking for cactuses."

"It's too wet here for cactuses," said Flyer. "All of my friends here live in the ocean like Garibaldi the fish and Rose the sea anemone."

"Hey look," Baloosh shouted excitedly, looking down through the clear water. "There's Dropsy, taking a nap."

"Shhhh," said Manoosh swimming with Flyer. "We shouldn't wake him up if he's tired. Anyway we should get going. We still have to find Nuno's home."

"It was nice to meet you, Flyer," Nuno said. "I hope we'll come back and visit you soon."

Everyone said goodbye and the three friends set off again.

"Hey, I think we're back in Rainbowland," said Baloosh.

A strong wind started blowing and Manoosh landed the balloon. They saw some large horns sticking up from behind a bush.

"What's that?" asked Baloosh.

"Let's go see," said Manoosh.

"It's Madame Butterfly," Nuno called out, "the most famous longhorn in Sonora. We're home!"

"Why Nuno," said the cow. "Where have you been? I know some cactuses who will be mighty happy to see you."

"Let's have a welcome home party for everyone," Liza the lizard said.

After the fiesta, Manoosh and Baloosh said goodbye to Nuno and flew back to Rainbowville, a few miles away.

"We traveled so far to find Nuno's home and it was so close to Rainbowville," said Baloosh.

"Yes, we did take the long way," said Manoosh. "But we made a good friend."

"And had a great adventure," added Baloosh. "I wouldn't have missed it for the world."

"Me either!" said Manoosh.

THE END

Lavinia's World is a company dedicated to children
and to their families. Our aim is to teach children about
the world around them and make learning fun.
Proceeds from the sale of Lavinia's World products
benefit children's causes.

Lavinia's World
titles available

The Little Stories of Manoosh and Baloosh

Make a Friend
Going Home
Bird Song

Softi's Adventures
The King of New York
Mission in Space
All Aboard!

The Kyss Family Mysteries
The Mystery of the Lost Bells
The Treasure of Lodian
The Great Paua Mystery

For a limited time only, collect all nine books, and
send in proof of purchase seals with a return address
to receive a free gift from Lavinia's World.
1100 Madison Avenue, Suite 3K-L, New York, New York 10028.
Visit our website for more information and fun stuff.
www.LaviniasWorld.com